MARY HOFFMAN has written over 90 books for children and in 1998 was made an Honorary Fellow of the Library Association for services to children and libraries. She is also the editor of the online quarterly children's book review *Armadillo*. In 1992 *Amazing Grace* was selected for Children's Book of the Year, Commended for the Kate Greenaway Medal and added to the National Curriculum Reading List, becoming an international best-seller. It was followed by *Grace & Family* and three Grace story books: *Starring Grace, Encore, Grace!* and *Bravo, Grace!* Mary's many other books for Frances Lincoln include *The Colour of Home, The Great Big Book of Feelings, The Great Big Book of Families,* and the soon-to-be published *Welcome to the Family*. Mary lives near Oxford. Find out more at www.maryhoffman.co.uk

CAROLINE BINCH's illustrations for *Hue Boy*, written by Rita Phillips Mitchell, won the Smarties Prize in 1993. She is perhaps best known for her illustrations for *Amazing Grace* and *Grace & Family*. *Gregory Cool*, which she both wrote and illustrated, was shortlisted for the Kate Greenaway Medal. It was followed by *Since Dad Left*, which won the United Kingdom Book Award in 1998, *Chenny's Dream* and *Silver Shoes*. Caroline lives in Cornwall.

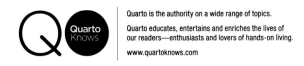

Quarto is the authority on a wide range of topics.

Quarto educates, entertains and enriches the lives of our readers—enthusiasts and lovers of hands-on living.

www.quartoknows.com

For Buchi Emecheta – M.H.
For Joe – C.B.

First published in Great Britain in 1991 by
Frances Lincoln Children's Books,
74-77 White Lion Street, London, N1 9PF
www.franceslincoln.com

First published in paperback in 2007

British Library Cataloguing in Publication Data available on request

ISBN 978-1-84507-749-5

Manufactured in Shenzhen, China RD 102017

19 18

MIX
Paper from
responsible sources
FSC® C101537

Amazing Grace

Mary Hoffman
Illustrated by Caroline Binch

F

FRANCES LINCOLN
CHILDREN'S BOOKS

Grace was a girl who loved stories.

She didn't mind if they were read to her or told to her or made up in her own head. She didn't care if they were from books or on TV or in films or on the video or out of Nana's long memory. Grace just loved stories.

And after she had heard them, or sometimes while they were still going on, Grace would act them out. And she always gave herself the most exciting part.

Grace went into battle as Joan of Arc . . .

and wove a wicked web as Anansi the spiderman.

She hid inside the wooden horse at the gates of Troy . . .

she crossed the Alps with Hannibal and a hundred elephants . . .

she sailed the seven seas
with a peg-leg
and a parrot.

She was Hiawatha, sitting by the shining Big-Sea-Water

and Mowgli in the back garden jungle.

But most of all Grace loved to act pantomimes. She
liked to be Dick Whittington turning to hear the
bells of London Town or Aladdin rubbing the
magic lamp. The best characters in pantomimes
were boys, but Grace played them anyway.

When there was no-one else around, Grace played
all the parts herself. She was a cast of thousands.
Paw-Paw the cat usually helped out.

And sometimes she could persuade Ma and Nana
to join in, when they weren't too busy. Then she
was Doctor Grace and their lives were in her hands.

One day at school her teacher said they were going to do the play of *Peter Pan*. Grace put up her hand to be . . . Peter Pan.

"You can't be called Peter," said Raj. "That's a boy's name."

But Grace kept her hand up.

"You can't be Peter Pan," whispered Natalie. "He wasn't black." But Grace kept her hand up.

"All right," said the teacher. "Lots of you want to be Peter Pan, so we'll have to have auditions. We'll choose the parts next Monday."

When Grace got home, she seemed rather sad.

"What's the matter?" asked Ma.

"Raj said I couldn't be Peter Pan because I'm a girl."

"That just shows all Raj knows about it," said Ma. "Peter Pan is *always* a girl!"

Grace cheered up, then later she remembered
something else. "Natalie says I can't be Peter Pan
because I'm black," she said.

Ma started to get angry but Nana stopped her.

"It seems that Natalie is another one who don't
know nothing," she said. "You can be anything
you want, Grace, if you put your mind to it."

Next day was Saturday and Nana told Grace they were going out. In the afternoon they caught a bus and a train into town. Nana took Grace to a grand theatre. Outside it said, "ROSALIE WILKINS in ROMEO AND JULIET" in beautiful sparkling lights.

"Are we going to the ballet, Nana?" asked Grace.
"We are, Honey, but I want you to look at these pictures first."
Nana showed Grace some photographs of a beautiful young girl dancer in a tutu. "STUNNING NEW JULIET!" it said on one of them.

"That one is little Rosalie from back home in Trinidad," said Nana. "Her Granny and me, we grew up together on the island. She's always asking me do I want tickets to see her little girl dance – so this time I said yes."

After the ballet, Grace played the part of Juliet,
dancing around her room in her imaginary tutu.
"I can be anything I want," she thought. "I can
even be Peter Pan."

On Monday they had the auditions. Their teacher let the class vote on the parts. Raj was chosen to play Captain Hook. Natalie was going to be Wendy.

Then they had to choose Peter Pan.

Grace knew exactly what to do – and all the words to say. It was a part she had often played at home. All the children voted for her.

"You were great," said Natalie.

The play was a great success and Grace was an
amazing Peter Pan.

After it was all over, she said, "I feel as if I could
fly all the way home!"

"You probably could," said Ma.

"Yes," said Nana. "If Grace put her mind to it –
she can do anything she want."

MORE GRACE TITLES FROM
FRANCES LINCOLN CHILDREN'S BOOKS

Grace & Family
Mary Hoffman
Illustrated by Caroline Binch
To Grace, family has always meant her Ma, her Nana and her cat Paw-Paw,
so when Papa invites her to visit him in the Gambia, she dreams of
finding a family straight out of one of her story books.
But, as Grace soon finds out, families are what you make them.
A warm and delightful follow-up to the international best-seller and modern classic, *Amazing Grace*.

Princess Grace
Mary Hoffman
Illustrated by Cornelius van Wright and Ying-Hwa Hu
Grace is back! The girl from *Amazing Grace* who proved that you can be
anything you want and that families are what you make them,
now discovers that there's more than one way to be a princess.
Grace has the chance to be a princess in a school parade. But what does a princess do,
apart from wearing beautiful clothes and looking pretty?

Starring Grace
Mary Hoffman
Grace the Explorer, Grace the Detective, Grace the Astronaut, Grace the Doctor…
In this high-spirited story book, Grace, the heroine of Mary Hoffman's
classic picture book, *Amazing Grace,* joins her friends Aimee, Kester,
Raj and Maria in a series of dramatic holiday adventures,
using her imagination to become just about anything she wants.

Frances Lincoln titles are available from all good bookshops.
You can also buy books and find out more about your favourite titles,
authors and illustrators on our website: www.franceslincoln.com